SAY A LITTLE
PRAYER

DIONNE WARWICK,

David Freeman Wooley, and Tonya Bolden

Illustrations by Soud

RP|KIDS
PHILADELPHIA • LONDON

Acknowledgments

I would like to thank all the wonderful people who worked on this project, including Running Press and the Perseus Books Group. A special thanks to Dave Wooley and his family. Dedication to my entire family, my sister, my sons, and all six of my grandchildren, and all those who believed this could be done. Last of all, thanks to all of you, my little and big readers. Remember, if you can think it—you can do it!

—Dionne Warwick

© 2008 by Dionne Warwick, David Freeman Wooley, Tonya Bolden
Illustrations © 2008 Dionne Warwick, David Freeman Wooley, Tonya Bolden

Printed in China

9 8 7 6 5 4 3 2 1
Digit on the right indicates the number of this printing.

Library of Congress Control Number: 2007935775

ISBN 978-0-7624-3268-4

Concept created by Dionne Warwick and David Freeman Wooley;
Text by Dionne Warwick and Tonya Bolden

Illustrations by Soud
Edited by Greg Jones
Typography: Bickley Script and Agenda

Published by Running Press Kids, an imprint of
Running Press Book Publishers
2300 Chestnut Street
Philadelphia, PA 19103-4371

Visit us on the web!
www.runningpress.com
www.dionnewarwick.info

Little D—that's me!
Up early to fix my hair,
and noodle about what jeans, jumper, or dress to wear.

After some oatmeal,
I'm off to school!

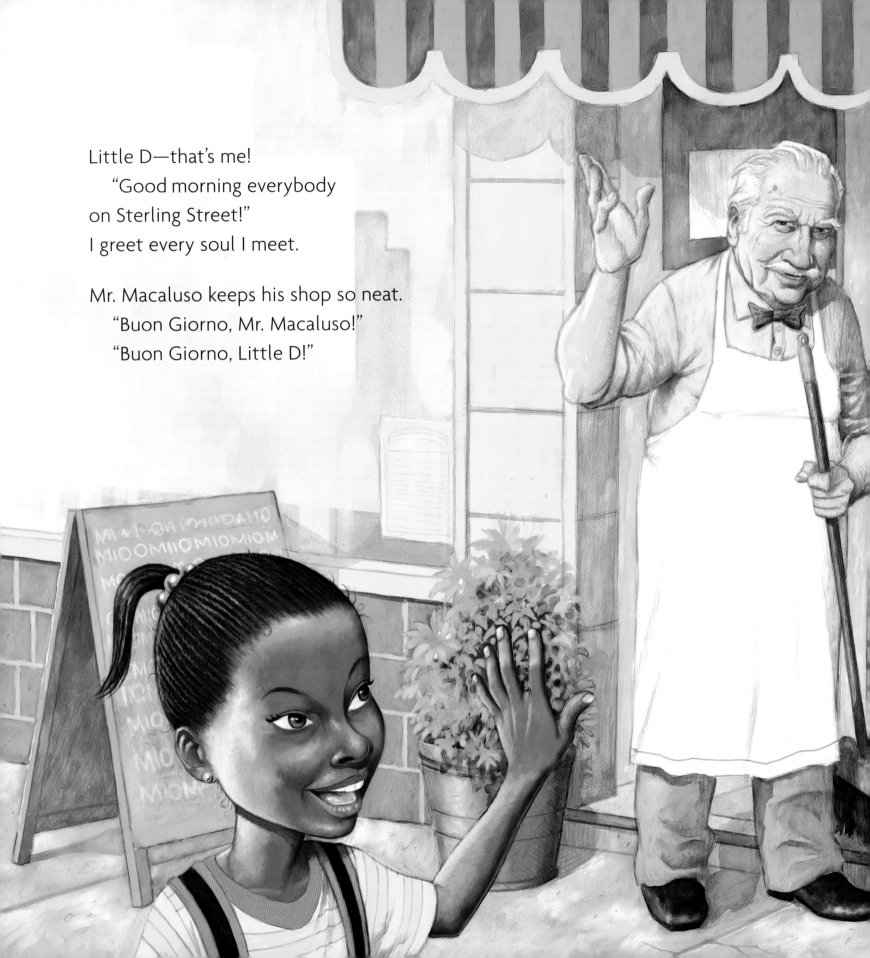

Little D—that's me!
   "Good morning everybody
on Sterling Street!"
I greet every soul I meet.

Mr. Macaluso keeps his shop so neat.
   "Buon Giorno, Mr. Macaluso!"
   "Buon Giorno, Little D!"

Mrs. Chavez has a Chihuahua named Pete.
"Buenas dias, Mrs. Chavez!"
"Buenas dias, Little D!"

"Good morning, Mr. Simon, Mr. Sullivan, Mrs. Sleet."
She looks a little grumpy, but she's really very sweet.

"Good morning, Little D!"
"Good morning, Little D!"
"Good morning, Little D!"

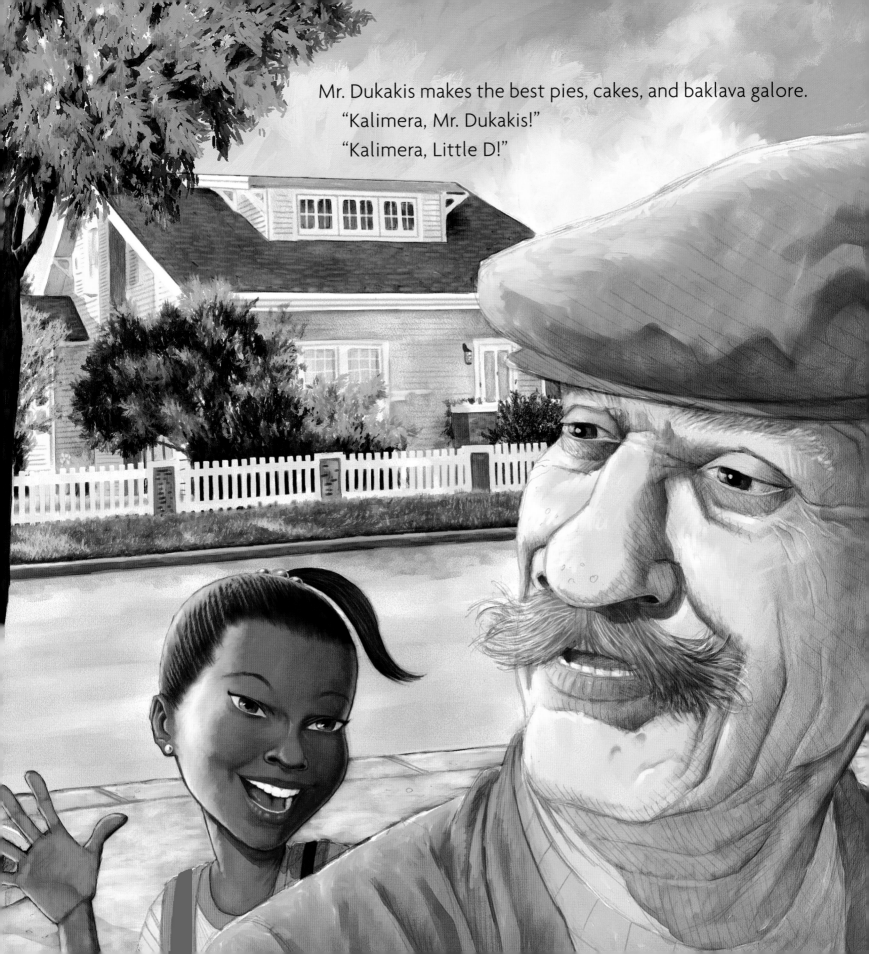

Mr. Dukakis makes the best pies, cakes, and baklava galore.
"Kalimera, Mr. Dukakis!"
"Kalimera, Little D!"

Right next door is Daddy's candy store!
No chocolates, caramels, or treats for me
til after three.

Little D—that's me!
I'm loving every hour of school—math the most.

Little D—that's me!
Later in the day, my homework's done.
Time for fun.

Basketball?
Stoopball?
Kickball?

Sometimes it's too hard to pick a game to play.
Maybe some of each before the sun says,
"Adios," for the day?

Plus, I have a treasure chest of pranks,
for hiding one of my brother's toys,
or
my sister's left shoe,
or
dressing our bow-bow,
   Sonny Boy,
in my fabulicious tutu.

Little D—that's me!
I'm happy to be myself.

When I feel creative,
I make a poem or
a little look-alike of my home
from clay.

When I feel adventurous,
I take pretend trips by train—*chug-a-lugga, chug-a-lugga,*
    by boat—*swish-swash, swish-swash*
    by plane—*zip-zoom, zip-zoom!*

to places I'm wishing
and hoping to go someday:
    London,
    Tokyo,
    Paris,
    Frankfurt,
    Rome,
    Abu Dhabi, and San Jose.

Little D—that's me!
I'm window-wishing
on a rainy day
about grown-up me.

Maybe I'll be a court stenographer,
getting the inside scoop on the law with
all its twists and turns.

Or, maybe I'll be a teacher.
(I love sharing what I learn.)

Or, maybe . . .
A ballet dancer!
Oooh! Watch me twirl!

*Does God want me to be
any of those things?* I ask myself.

Little D—that's me!
I'm feeling SHOCKED
when Grandpa made a surprise request
    one Sunday Morning.

The choir had sung "Rock of Ages" and
    "Nearer My God to Thee."
It was time for Grandpa to preach, but instead,
    he beckoned for me.

What could Grandpa want?
I wondered on my way up front.
    "Little D, I would like for you to sing,"
he said.

Grandpa had that knowing look in his eyes.
Daddy calls it Grandpa's look of
　　RE-VE-LA-TION
　　and
　　IN-SPI-RA-TION!

Suddenly, the whole church was clapping
and cheering me on. I wasn't just shocked. I was nervous.
　"Grandpa?" I whispered,
"Do you really think I can sing?"

"I sure do! And if *you* can think it, *you* can do it, Little D,"
he replied, with a
    RE-VE-LA-TION
    and
    IN-SPI-RA-TION smile.

Grandpa always said that to folks who came to him for counsel and hope.
But on that Sunday morning, when I looked up into Grandpa's wise eyes,
I felt the power of those words for the first time—for *me,* Little D.

"If you can think it, you can do it." I whispered.
"I'll say a little prayer for you," Grandpa promised.

I said a little prayer, too.
I closed my eyes and started singing "Jesus Loves Me"
with all my might,
moving through the notes just right.

I felt so free, I felt so . . . fully me!
I couldn't believe all that applause was for me,
Little D.

When Grandpa preached, he said
"God blesses everybody with many talents and smiles
when we use our gifts for good.
Our lives rise when we find and let shine our top talent.
It's the one that brings you the most joy."
"*Never ever* be sloppy with your talents," he added.
"Always treat them with extra special care and prayer."

It felt like Grandpa was talking just to me.

I knew right then, right there, that nothing—
no ball game, no poem,
no amount of play with clay,
no pretend trips,
not even math or ballet class—
had ever filled me with such soul-deep joy
as when I gave myself to song that Sunday.

Little D—that's me!
Practice! **Practice! Practice!**

I practice singing melodies note for note.
    I make sure not to strain my throat.
I practice keeping in sync with the beat.
    It helps if you pat your feet.

Always, before I practice, I say a little prayer.

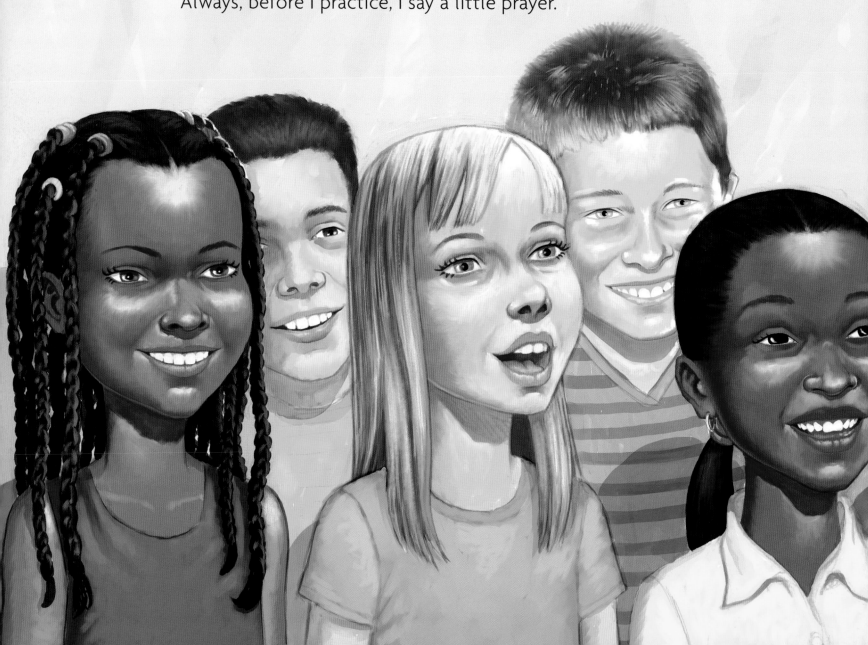

You see, now I'm in two choirs—
    the choir at church and the choir at school.
If I find another one, I might join that choir, too.
In just a few days, I'll be singing someplace new!

Little D—that's me!, with Daddy taking my picture outside the world-famous Apollo Theater in Harlem, New York City. That's many, many miles away from Sterling Street.

After Mommy heard about the Apollo's Amateur Night for Kids, my whole family said, "Little D, you must sing in that show!"

Even Sonny Boy let loose happy woof-woofs.

I could think it.
I could do it.

I said a little prayer before
I stepped on stage.

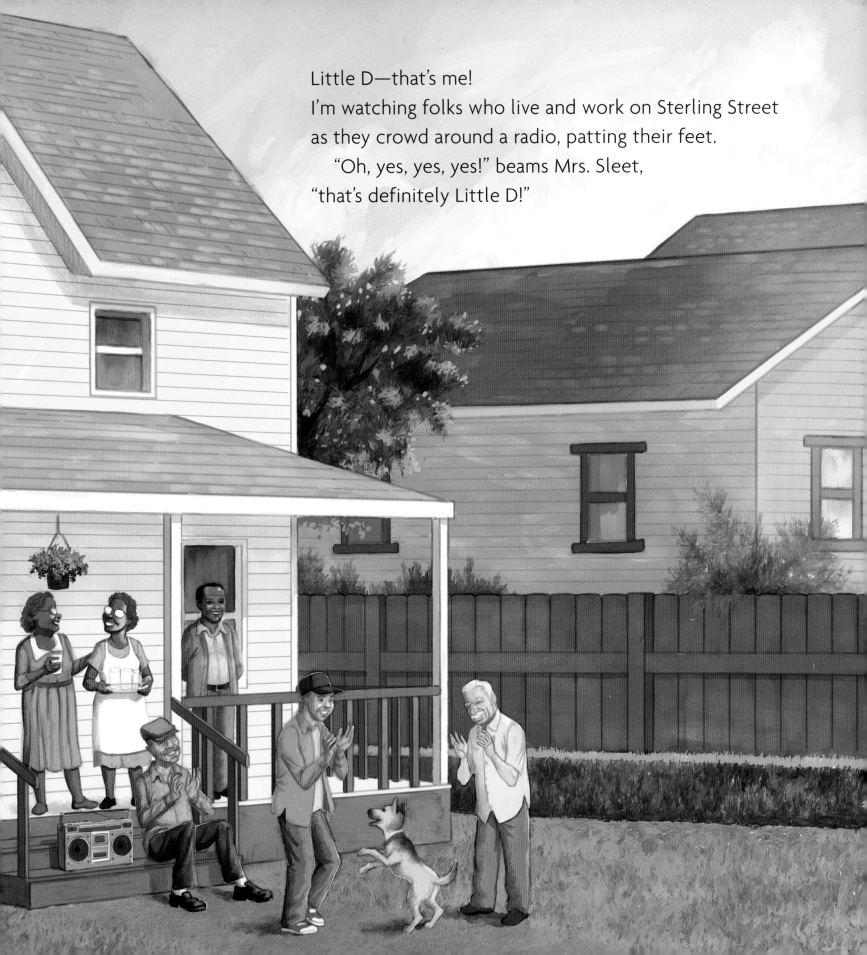

Little D—that's me!
I'm watching folks who live and work on Sterling Street
as they crowd around a radio, patting their feet.
  "Oh, yes, yes, yes!" beams Mrs. Sleet,
"that's definitely Little D!"

As for me, Little D, I say a little prayer for
YOU, **YOU, YOU.**

May you find your top talent, your soul-deep joy.
May you *never ever* let it go.